Number Three

Dorling Kinderlsey
www.dk.com

Editor Fiona Munro
Designer Lisa Hollis

Published in Great Britain in 1997
by Dorling Kindersley Limited, 9 Henrietta St, London WC2E 8PS
This edition published in 2000

A CIP catalogue record for this book is available from the British Library.

ISBN 0-7513-6703-6

Color reproduction by DOT Gradations
Printed in Hong Kong by Wing King Tong

Number Three

COLIN AND JACQUI HAWKINS

Dorling Kindersley

"It's wonderful being me," said Number Three.

"But I can't remember why!"
Number Three lived in
the third house in Numbertown.
It was a little red house with three blue
chimney-pots and three yellow windows.
The address was 3, Number Lane.

Number Three had
three teddy bears,
three kites,
three balls,
three toy boats,
and three toy cars.

Time for tea.

He kept them all
in three toy boxes.
He also had three alarm clocks,
because he always forgot
what time it was.

One day, while Number Three was out walking in Numbertown, it rained and rained and rained.

Oh no!

"Oh silly me," said Number Three.

"I forgot all three of my umbrellas."
He got very wet.

"Attishoo! Attishoo! Attishoo!"

Number Three sneezed home to bed.
"I don't feel well," he sniffed miserably.
He used up three whole boxes of tissues.

After three days, Number Three
felt a lot better. He didn't need his
three hot water bottles anymore.

He got up and had three showers.
He used three bars of soap.

Squeak! Squeak! Squeak!

"I'm squeaky clean now!" he sang happily.

Number Three was eating his breakfast when
three letters popped through the letterbox.
He quickly tore them open.
They were birthday cards!

"Oh silly me,"
said Number Three.

"I forgot my own birthday!"
Number Three decided to bake
three birthday cakes and have a party.

He stirred the cake mixture and then poured it into three round cake tins. He popped them into the hot oven.

Three hours later, Number Three smelled something burning.

Sniff! Sniff! Sniff!

"What's cooking?" he thought. "Oh no! I forgot the cakes!" All three cakes were burnt.

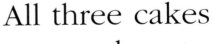
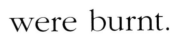
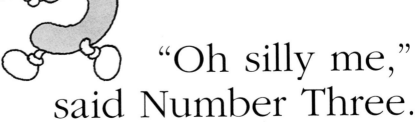

"Oh silly me," said Number Three.

"Now I'll have to go and buy a birthday cake," sighed Number Three.

I'll scoot along.

He hopped onto his scooter,
and three minutes later he was whizzing
past the swings in Numbertown Park.
"That looks fun," said Number Three.
"I must have a go!"

"Happy birthday to me,"
sang Number Three.

Number Three had a wonderful time.
"I can fly!" he cried,
swinging through the air.

Time for a spin!

Then Number Three had
three long rides on the roundabout.
"I feel dizzy," he giggled.

It was so much fun, he forgot the time.

"Happy birthday to me,"
sang Number Three.

Bong! Bong! Bong!

chimed the Numbertown clock.

"Oh silly me,"
said Number Three.

He jumped on his scooter and sped to the
cake shop. It had closed at three o'clock.
Number Three set off sadly towards home.
He wondered what to do.

Number Three pushed
open the door.
"Happy birthday to you!"
shouted Numberlies
One and Two.
They gave Number Three
a big birthday cake
and three presents.
He blew out the candles
and wished three wishes.
"How old are you?" asked Number One
as they all tucked into the cake.

"Oh silly me,"
said Number Three.
"I've forgotten!"